If I Were A Frog

For Zachary!
Frog On!
Sherry Been

by Sherry Been
Illustrations by M. Angels

Dedicated to my grandmother

Book Design by R. Rosenzweig

Printed in Hong Kong

ISBN: 0-9705693-0-0

Guaranteed Trade Binding

This Frogbook belongs to:

Luis

If I were a frog,
I would sit on a log,
and snack all night and day.

And if you should ask
on what I would snack,
this is what I would say:

While worms and slugs are very good grub,
beetles and ants also enchant.

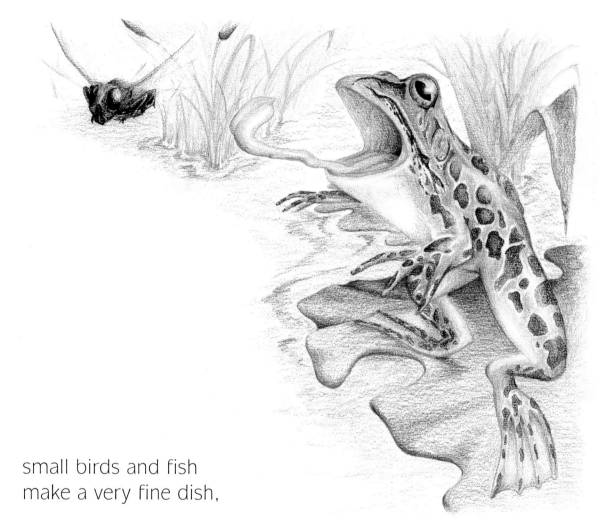

small birds and fish
make a very fine dish,

...but flies are the best
of all the rest.

My tongue is attached to the front of my mouth.
When I see food, it swiftly flicks out.

Escaping would be extremely tricky,
because my tongue is very sticky.

NOW THAT YOU KNOW WHAT I LIKE TO EAT,

LET'S FIND OUT WHAT LIKES TO EAT ME.

It's the fish
that like to boast,
"We're the ones
who eat frogs most."

Lots of creatures, like
raccoons and snakes,
think what a great meal
a frog would make.

And though I consider it terribly rude,

other frogs like to eat me too.

People raise me on farms
for my legs they eat.
I'm considered delicious
for my tender meat.

NOW THAT YOU KNOW WHAT LIKES TO EAT ME,

LET'S FIND OUT HOW I CAME TO BE.

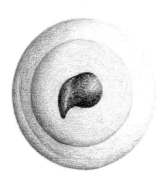

Frog spawn is what you call frog eggs
before they start to hatch.
There are usually several hundred
in each and every batch.

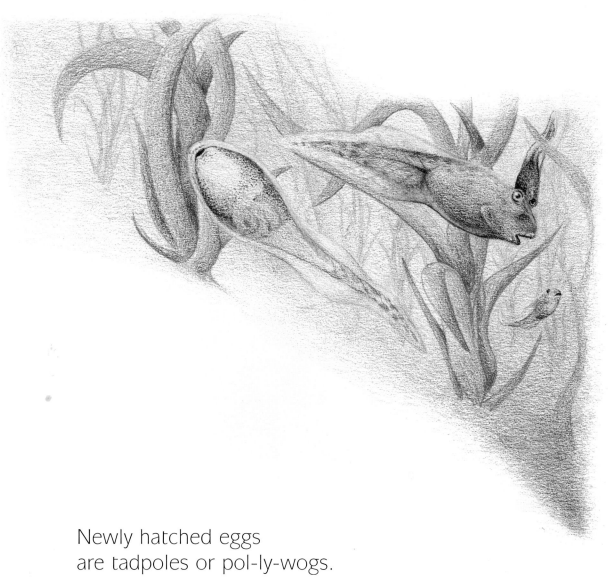

Newly hatched eggs
are tadpoles or pol-ly-wogs.
It's called meta-mor-pho-sis
as we change into frogs.

When we change to a frog our tail disappears.
Then we grow lungs, and legs, and ears.

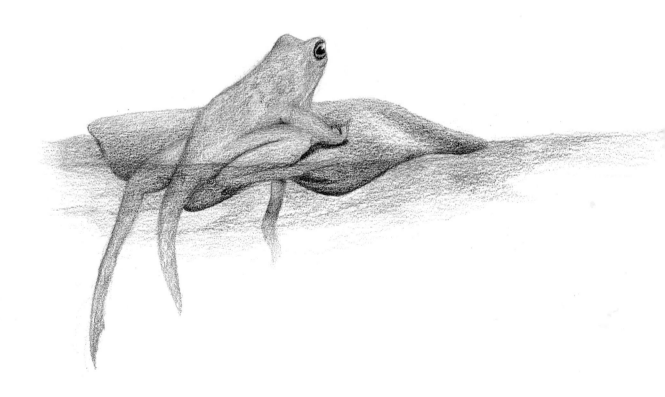

Some frogs hatch
inside a pouch.
Some even hatch in their
mother's mouth.

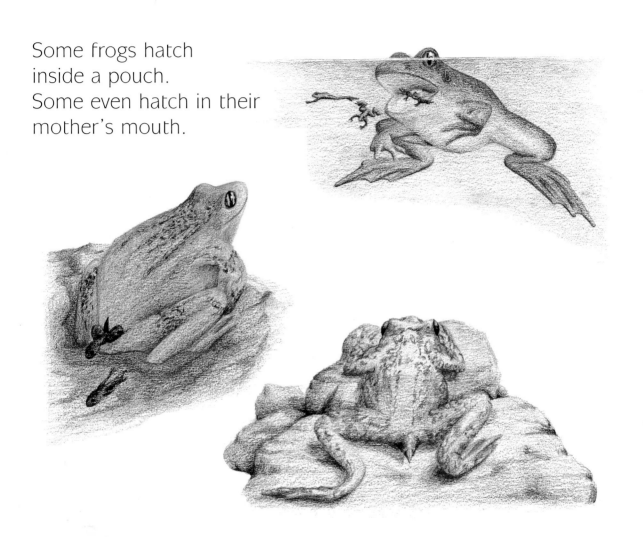

Other frogs miss that tadpole stage.
They start out as frogs at a very young age.

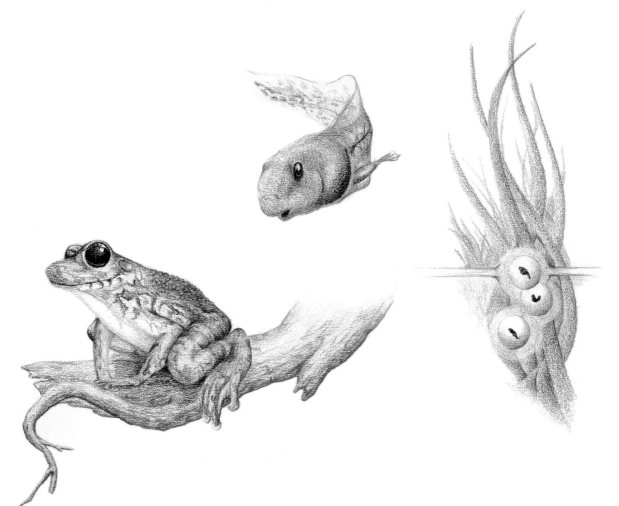

NOW THAT YOU KNOW HOW I CAME TO BE,

LET'S LEARN ABOUT MY ANATOMY.

Most frogs have legs
that are really quite long.

We can jump very far
because our legs are so strong.

When we are scared
we jump quickly away.

Yet stay very still
when hunting for prey.

When frogs swim, we really can go.
This is because we have webbed toes.

Frog eyes never move.
They look like a cat's.

Our bodies must face
what we're looking at.

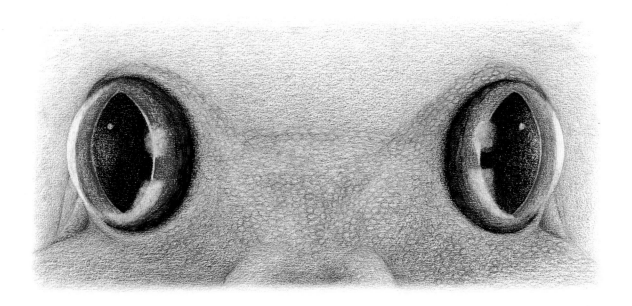

Frog skin is smooth,
and looks quite shiny.
It feels very slippery
and super slimy.

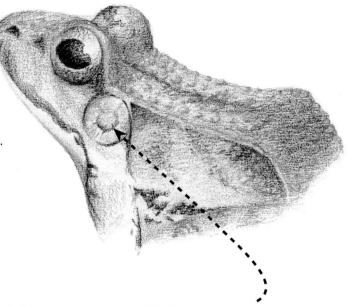

Though frogs have teeth,
they're really quite useless.

We might as well
have grown up toothless.

Behind frog eyes you'll find our ears.
Sounds are easy for us to hear.

NOW THAT YOU KNOW MY ANATOMY,

LET'S FIND OUT WHAT MAKES ME BE ME.

Living in water and living on land,
the species of frogs is am-phi-bi-an.

Amphibians are really wonderful creatures,
here are more of our fabulous features:

We don't drink water
in the usual way.
Instead we sit
in water all day.

The water is absorbed
right through our skin.
It's very helpful
our skin is so thin.

Croaking and squeaking is our way of speaking.

Our throats fill with air, and it echoes around.
This is what makes that unique frog sound.

By listening we know when a frog of our own
is calling on us to come back home.

Frogs are cold-blooded
with a three-chambered heart.
We sit in the sun
to warm all our parts.

When it turns cold
frogs hy-ber-nate.
Our breathing slows down
to a very slow rate.

Frogs freeze like a rock
when the weather is freezing.
When it thaws out,
we re-start our breathing.

In the summer when it's hot and dry,
frogs must have water
or we'll probably die.

We build a cocoon way underground.
This gives needed moisture
'till the rains come around.

We protect ourselves
in unusual ways,
and use these devices
every day.

We can swell
to twice our size.
This can be
a scary disguise.

Some frogs secrete mucus
from poisonous glands.

Our enemies re-think
their dining plans.

We can change colors
or look like a tree.
This makes it harder
for us to be seen.

Frogs are nocturnal, sleeping most the day.
We wake up and eat the night away.

NOW THAT YOU KNOW WHAT MAKES ME BE ME,

LET'S LEARN ABOUT FROG VARIETIES.

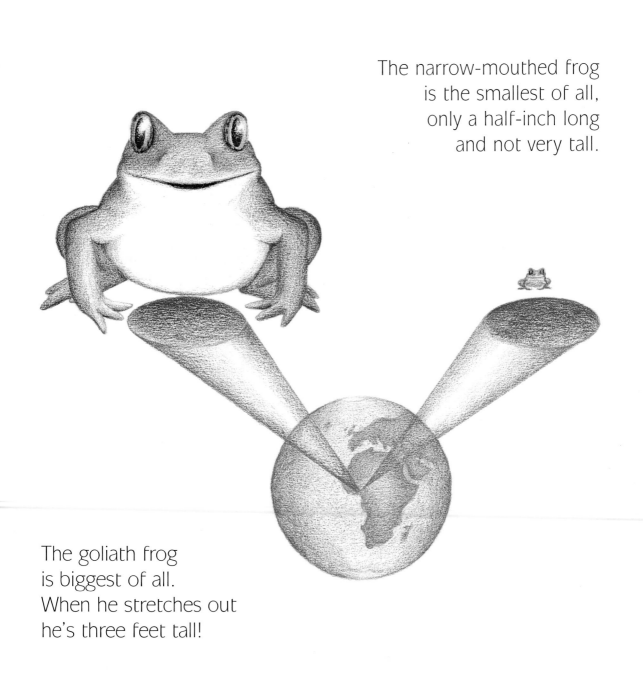

The narrow-mouthed frog
is the smallest of all,
only a half-inch long
and not very tall.

The goliath frog
is biggest of all.
When he stretches out
he's three feet tall!

The tree frog sleeps
for most of the day.
He comes out at night
to stalk his prey.

He only jumps when he must,
and walks along tree parts
as soon as it's dusk.

On a tree branch he will linger,
because of suction pads
on his toes and fingers.

Arrow poison dart frogs
that are pretty and bright,
raise tadpoles in branches
way out of sight.

Tiny glass frogs
have clear looking skin.
You can see their green bones
when you look at them.

Toads are frogs too,
all brown and warty.
They often live until the age of forty!

A toad's skin is dry and not very shiny.
Their legs are short, so their steps are tiny.

A Suranum toad has a spongelike back.
This is where her eggs will hatch.

The cane toad is
as mean as can be.
He lives in Australia
down under the trees.

As you can see,
there is much to know.

Like how frogs are born,
and how we grow.

So thank you for reading
my book about frogs.

Now I must go
and sit on a log.

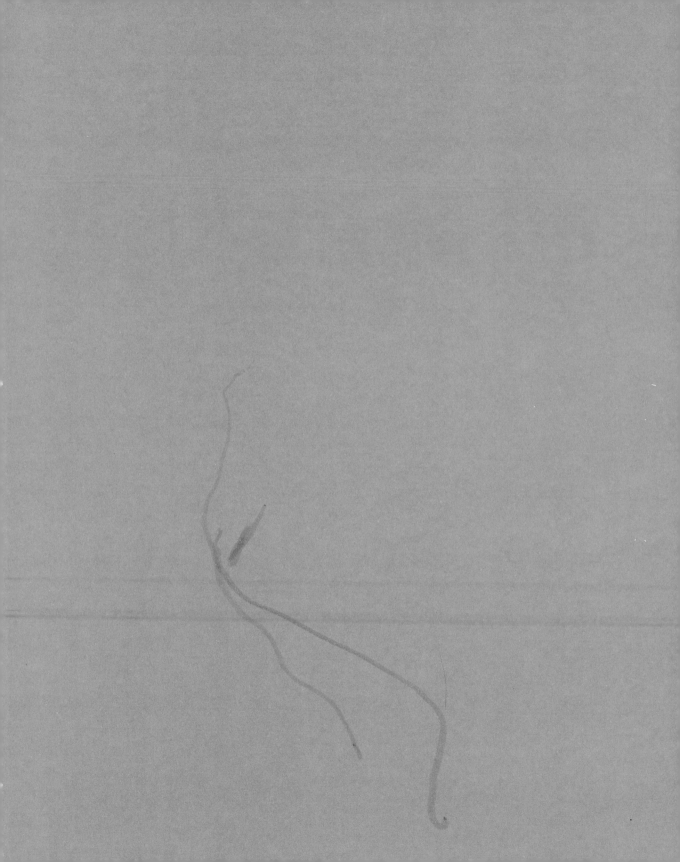